WE CAN READ!™

Meadow Magic

by Jacqueline Sweeney

photography by G. K. & Vikki Hart
photo illustration by Blind Mice Studio

BENCHMARK BOOKS

MARSHALL CAVENDISH
NEW YORK

For Peggy, Linda, Bev, and Jude,
who understand the magic

With thanks to Daria Murphy, reading specialist and
principal of Scotchtown Elementary, Goshen, New York,
for reading this manuscript with care and for writing the
"We Can Read and Learn" activity guide.

Benchmark Books
Marshall Cavendish
99 White Plains Road
Tarrytown, New York 10591-9001
Website:www.marshallcavendish.com

Text copyright © 2002 by Jacqueline Sweeney
Photo illustrations © 2002 by G.K. & Vikki Hart
and Mark and Kendra Empey

Library of Congress Cataloging-in-Publication Data
Sweeney, Jacqueline.
Meadow Magic /by Jacqueline Sweeney.
p.   cm. — (We can read!)
Summary: Hildy the duck helps Ladybug prepare
to sing at the Big Bug Concert.
ISBN 0-7614-1124-0
[1. Singing—Fiction. 2. Ladybugs—Fiction. 3. Ducks—Fiction.
4. Insects—Fiction. 5. Friendship—Fiction.] I. Title.
PZ7.S974255 Me 2001   [E]—dc21   00-140124

Printed in Italy

1 3 5 6 4 2

Characters

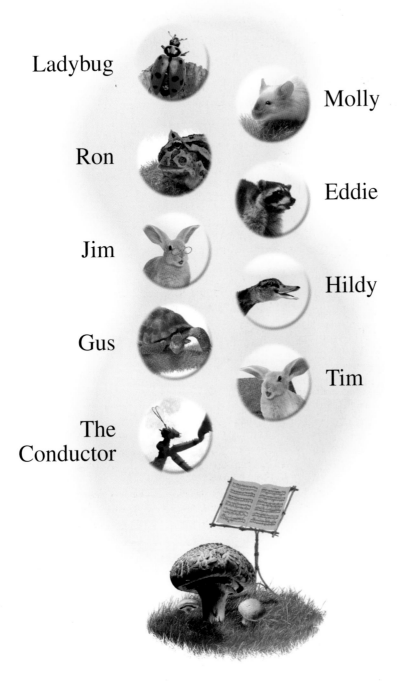

Ladybug

Molly

Ron

Eddie

Jim

Hildy

Gus

Tim

The
Conductor

Me

Me   *Me*

Me   *Me*

Whatʼs that awful sound?" asked Molly.

"Ladybug is singing," croaked Ron.

"She has a solo in the Big Bug Concert."

"She's squeaking," moaned Eddie.

"How can we help her?" asked Jim.

"The concert is in five days!" said Molly.

"And none of *us* knows how to sing."

"I do!" quacked Hildy.

"I was born to sing."

She lifted her beak and sang:

Ladybug, Ladybug

Sing out your song

With Hildy's help

You'll never go wrong!

Ma

Ma   Ma

Ma   Ma

"Oh dear," said Hildy.

"We'd better get started."

Ladybug hopped on her back.

Off they swam to a quiet spot.

And so, Ladybug's lessons began.

Hildy taught her how to stand up tall and hold the music low.

She showed her how to sing loud and soft and fast and slow.

At first they sang together.

They sang to the pond,

to the sky,

to the leaves and rocks.

Then Ladybug sang by herself,
to the clouds, to the sunset,
to the stars and the moon.

"At last," quacked Hildy,
"You're in tune!"

On the fifth day, Hildy said,
"Ladybug, you're ready.
Hurry up, it's time to go!"
They raced to Pond Rock.

The friends were waiting.

Gus gave Ladybug a music stand.
Eddie gave her his lucky feather.

Then they all walked together
to the Big Bug Concert
in the meadow.

The grass was glowing with fireflies.
Horns and strings and reeds and drums
were tuning up to play.

Tap, tap, tap, went the conductor's baton.
Suddenly the meadow was still.

The Crickets played first.

They played Mozart
and "Itsy Bitsy Spider."

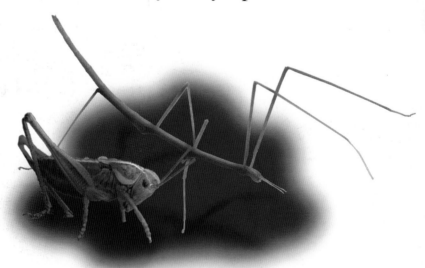

Grasshopper and Walking Stick joined in.
Everyone clapped at the end.

Tap, tap, tap, went the baton.

"Here comes Ladybug," whispered Ron.

Ladybug bowed,

Then she stood up tall.

She sang to the meadow.

She sang to the trees.

She sang to the moonlight.

She sang to the breeze.

When the song was over
everyone clapped and cheered.

Ladybug got daisies.
All the bugs went wild.
"Bravo!" they shouted.

Ladybug left the stage.
She walked down the aisle
and handed her daisies to Hildy.

The
End

WE CAN READ AND LEARN

The following activities are designed to enhance literacy development. *Meadow Magic* can help children build skills in vocabulary, phonics, and creative writing; explore self-awareness; and make connections between literature and other subject areas such as science and math.

LADYBUGS'S CHALLENGE WORDS

There are many challenging vocabulary words in this story. At the Big Bug Concert, Ladybug sang "to the meadow... to the trees... to the moonlight... to the breeze." Help Ladybug sing. Have children make up a song for her, using as many words as they can from the list below. Look at the second list of rhyming words and ask children to include as many of them as possible.

awful	sound	solo	concert
moan	beak	wrong	start
quiet	swam	lessons	taught
low	together	clouds	aisle
sunset	tune	feather	conductor
baton	crickets	moonlight	stage

RHYMING WORDS

me/we/she
song/wrong
oh/so/go
low/slow/show/glow
moon/tune
day/they
do/to/you
itsy/bitsy
Ron/baton
clap/tap
tall/all
trees/breeze

FUN WITH PHONICS

The sounds of words are important for children to learn. Children can draw different instruments that make special sounds, just as words do. Then, help them find words from the story that have the same vowel sound as the instrument. For example, on a picture of a drum, add words such as *us*, *bug*, *up*, and *lucky*. On a violin, add *in*, *sing*, *big*, and *lift*. On a clarinet, add *she*, *beak*, *leaves*, and so on.

When the word work is done, help children learn about the different musical instruments and the families of the orchestra. Try to plan a trip to a real concert.

SING TO THE MOON

Ladybug sings to the things in nature that she loves. Become a naturalist and help children study the sky. Choose one aspect of the sky (clouds, sun, moon, or stars) and research what it is made of, what it looks like, its size, color, shape, and so on. Children should cut out five to ten shapes that are representative of the element they have chosen (stars, circles for suns, crescents for moons, cloudlike puffs). On each, they should write one of the facts they have learned. Use the shapes to create a mural of the sky. Divide a sheet of construction or craft paper into two columns and write "day sky" on one side and "night sky" on the other. Put the shapes where they belong to create an informative and beautiful mural. Add other items that you might find, such as owls at night or birds in the day.

FEELING THE MEADOW MAGIC

The meadow held so much magic for Ladybug as she sang. Help children create their own story magic. Fold a plain sheet of white paper into thirds. Discuss with children how Ladybug felt at the beginning of the story. How did she feel in the middle? The end? Children can draw pictures that correspond to the parts of the story and write a simple sentence about each one. Sequencing the events will improve comprehension skills.

About the author

Jacqueline Sweeney is a poet and children's author. She has worked with children and teachers for over twenty-five years implementing writing workshops in schools throughout the United States. She specializes in motivating reluctant writers and shares her creative teaching methods in numerous professional books for teachers. She lives in Stone Ridge, New York.

About the photo illustrations

The photo illustrations are the collaborative effort of photographers G. K. and Vikki Hart and Blind Mice Studio. Following Mark Empey's sketched storyboard, G. K. and Vikki Hart photograph each animal and element individually. The images are then scanned and manipulated, pixel by pixel, by Mark and Kendra Empey at Blind Mice Studio.

Each charming illustration may contain from 15 to 30 individual photographs.

All the animals that appear in this book were handled with love. They have been returned to or adopted by loving homes.